something

like the

end

something

like the

end

stories by ashley morrow hermsmeier

Black
Lawrence
Press

Black
Lawrence
Press

www.blacklawrence.com

Executive Editor: Diane Goettel
Chapbook Editor: Kit Frick
Book and Cover Design: Amy Freels
Cover Art: "something like the end" (charcoal, watercolor, and pen) by
Miriam Amerling Haughey. Used with permission.

Published 2019 by Black Lawrence Press.
Printed in the United States.

For the strange and lonely.

Contents

When the Bees Come Back

Rayna used the last of the duct tape to seal up the kitchen window. She'd have to settle for packing tape on the front door. That is, if the handyman ever left—how long could it take to seal air vents? She wiped sweat from her upper lip.

He entered the kitchen. He wasn't a large man, yet he managed to fill the narrow passage.

"Welp, that's the last of 'em. Fingers crossed, those little buggers won't be bothering you. At least not from the ducts."

"How much do I owe you?"

"How 'bout a beer instead and we drink to life while we still got it," he said and laughed. She forced a laugh, out of kindness, and opened the refrigerator door between them. She'd have to make small talk now—why couldn't he just go?

"I have Corona or IPA—which do you prefer?" she said, smiling even though he couldn't see it. She thought of her mother: *Let me hear the smile in your voice*, she used to say.

"I love a cold blonde," he said. "Though a hot one like you's even better."

She rolled her eyes then stood up with the Coronas and gave each one a crack against the kitchen counter.

"Impressive," he said.

"I don't have any limes."

"To all the buzz about the end of the world," he said and laughed so hard the windows might have rattled if it weren't for all the tape and boards. They clinked bottles.

"You have anyone coming to sit with you when they pass through?" he asked.

"My family, all of them, lived—*live*—in Salinas. So . . ."

"Ah, shit," he said. "I'm sorry. Survivors?"

"Haven't heard yet"—she took a swig and blinked hard—"but you know . . . just want to get through the next twenty-four hours, then I'll drive up there and deal with it. What about you?"

"Aw, yeah. I'll probably go to my mom's house. I've got it all situated and sealed up. Haven't touched my place yet, so . . ."

"Better hurry. The swarm's only a few hours away, right—if the wind doesn't change?"

He didn't budge. "Have you thought about trying to outrun them?" he asked. "You've got the legs for it."

She smiled again, this time without her eyes. She shifted her weight and hid one leg behind the other, feeling exposed in her thin running shorts.

"I did actually." His eyes were steady on her, so she kept hers down as if studying the linoleum. "But, you know, the reports of people getting caught in their cars . . . just awful—so awful. I figure I'll just stay and listen to the reports, you know? At least that way I won't be taken by surprise out on the road. God, what a way to go."

"Sure-sure-sure."

He moved into the small kitchen. Rayna took a step back and leaned against the fridge.

"It sure is creepy once the houses are all sealed up like this, isn't it?" he said. "How everything is so muffled all of a sudden?"

"Like the snow," she said.

"How's that?"

"You know, like, how after a snow the world outside gets all quiet? Like, nature realizes how beautiful it is or something and just kind of stops talking."

"Nature stops talking, huh?"

"Well, you know what I mean. It's like the world knows sound would ruin it."

"Never been to the snow. Don't see the need for it," he said. "But I get it. Kinda like, right now: you know people are out there, but are they really? I mean, I don't hear any cars going by, do you? Nobody walking their dogs. Not even any planes overhead. Everyone's got themselves all locked up, sealed up tight in little boxes. Nobody in. Nobody out. Would we even hear the neighbors' screams if it all started going down right now? Would they hear ours? We could be the only two people alive right now for all the silence."

Rayna looked at the radio on the counter. She wanted to hear someone else's voice. To feel as if someone else were in the room with them.

What she really wanted was to hear that all those bees that disappeared so long ago weren't really coming back. That they weren't aggressive. That they weren't wiping out entire towns. That a single sting didn't mean death. She wanted to hear that Salinas was still standing. Fresno and Bakersfield and Visalia too. She wanted to hear that the world was right again. That it was safe once more. But it wasn't. And, really, had it ever been?

She reached for that other voice. He stepped in front of her and placed a hand on her arm. His fingers wrapped all the way around her bicep. His neck hadn't been shaved. He smelled of gasoline and something metallic. His grip tightened. A ringing in her ears. Maybe a buzz. This was how the world would end, not with the sound of a trillion wings pulsing through her brain, but by the storm standing over her.

His Adam's apple bobbed with the last gulps of beer. He set the bottle on the counter and lowered his face toward hers. "Be sure you seal that front door real good when I go."

The Big One

Day 1

It's hot, even at night. We sleep on top of our duvets and sweat under rattling ceiling fans. We live too close to the sea to be an air-conditioned city—that's what we tell ourselves.

Most of us are asleep when it happens. We roll over and some of us sigh a little and some of us mumble, *Did you feel that?* Some of our dogs growl or whine or bark, but that's nothing new to us.

In the morning we hear about the 3.2 on the morning news. We see the pictures now slightly askew—proof it happened even if we don't remember. We straighten them and are glad we use studfinders. We make coffee. We have breakfast. Those of us with kids beg them to get ready because, *No, school does not get canceled for earthquakes in the night.* Some of us kiss each other and go to work. We all get on with our day.

A water main bursts on Broadway. The courthouse will overlook a river for a while: parked cars for riverbanks, streetlights for trees, cigarette butts for bubbles in the eddies. We watch it on TV, the fire crews and flashing lights and city workers in waders. We shake our heads and say, *Look at all that water.*

Our kids come home from school shouting, *Did you feel all the aftershocks?* and we say, *Didn't feel a thing—you kids and your imaginations.*

The men and women on the nightly news show us pictures and videos of structural damages throughout the city so slight we laugh. *Why do they bother?* We've seen it all before.

Day 2

Our dogs are acting strange. They bark at curbs and walls and mailboxes on our walks. They tuck their tails and slink away from fire hydrants, from manholes, from storm drains. We can't make sense of it. *The Big One is coming*, a neighbor says. We nod, *Probably*. It's been on its way for as long as anyone can remember.

We turn on the TV and are told by scientists that the quake isn't over. That the instruments with all those lines and needles say the earthquake is still going. We look at one another. We hold our hands out in front of us; we squint our eyes and cock our heads and listen for the rumble that must be there, for the vibration that should be felt. We hear nothing, we feel nothing, but our dogs are pacing; they look out the windows as if someone were coming up the walk. We are told to keep our earthquake kits available, but responsible fault-liners like us keep them close always.

A car alarm goes off in the middle of the night. The wail of distant sirens seems to have no end. A dog is howling somewhere. This is new to us.

Day 3

At night we kick at sweaty sheets and curse the heat that binds our lungs. *Can't breathe*, we say. *The air is so heavy.* Our children complain and cry. *Isn't it fall yet*, we say in the dark. It's October. *It's The Great Pumpkin, Charlie Brown* and candied apples and scarves. It's not oscillating fans and ice-soaked rags and "Don't touch me; it's too hot," except, it is. We kick at our sheets some more. *This feels like the end of the world*, we say.

In the morning we gather in front of our homes and apartments. We look at each other, at the streets, at the sidewalks, and we point. *Was that crack there before? Do you feel anything?* Some of us, even those with creaky knees, press our ears to the Earth and say we can hear a hum—can hear Her belly rumble. Some of us say, *No, She's always sounded like that.*

We go about our day.

At lunch, the water in our glasses ripples. The forks resting on our plates buzz. Some of us feel like we stood up too fast.

The talking heads say seismologists are baffled—it's the same quake and it's still not done. They tell us to stay home now, to avoid driving over bridges or stopping under overpasses for now, just in case. *Just in case of what*, we ask. But we know.

We walk gentle. We talk quiet. We move with apology and ask the ground to stay right where it is.

Day 4

A sinkhole has opened up at the ballpark, and it's full of water. The heat continues and children ask if they can go swim in the Center-field Pond. *It's not safe*, we tell them, *it might swallow you whole. It might spit you out in China!* We joke but we don't laugh.

Business owners near the ballpark are interviewed on the evening news; they show us cracks in walls, doors that stick, windows that won't open. *The city is sinking*, one man says to the camera, and we look at each other and shake our heads. *The city can't be sinking.*

They would tell us if the city were sinking.

Day 5

The earthquake continues—so they say. We can't feel it, but it is there below us, happening. *Stay at home*, they tell us.

More sinkholes have opened in the night: one on westbound 8, another one downtown, and one in suburbia that swallowed a Volvo.

We are restless. We mill around outside. We look up at telephone polls and wonder what direction they might tip. We look at the trees and wonder at limbs we never noticed before. We estimate and gauge our distances; we calculate and plan our options. Garage doors are open and for a while we peer into each other's lives. We pull weeds out front, we squat over cracks in our driveways, we walk our shaking dogs and some of us ask... *about the Ehrenfelds? Their house has a low spot—pencils roll right off the coffee table. The Vandervorts? Yeah, it's their ceilings—floors are covered in dust. The Logans? Fence tipped over. And the Drieses, the Cranmores, the Gampels, yes everyone on Quimby, their front doors won't open—they have to go around back for now.*

If only it were cold. If only we didn't need our ceiling fans and windows open we could curl up under our blankets and feel in some ways less exposed. We might not hear the cracks and snaps of homes shifting off foundations. We might not hear windows shatter under all this tilted pressure. We might not hear the car alarms, the sirens, and the howling dogs.

We rest as best we can knowing tomorrow we'll get up to measure some more.

Day 6

Today someone wakes with a headache. With a stiff neck. With a cold. Someone digs a grave. Patches a hole. Sews a stitch. A girl asks a boy to dance.

A child goes down a slide. Eats lunch alone. Walks to the principal's office.

A man is fired. Gets promoted. Orders a drink. A man says to his wife, "I'm leaving you." "I love you." "Where are my socks?"

A woman is laid off. Gets hired. Orders a drink. A woman says to her husband, "I'm leaving you." "I love you." "Put on some socks."

Some shake cans on street corners. Sleep next to shopping carts. Shout at no one. At everyone. Fall down while crossing the street.

Today the Earth wakes up and swallows a man.

Day 7

The power has gone out. The mayor says, *Hang tight*, and in the next breath, *but if you have family to stay with, consider evacuation. It's temporary*, he says. *We'll get through this*, he says.

The neighbors' wives and children are leaving. *We'll be back when everything has settled*, they say. The fathers stay with the houses and pretend it will be over soon. Tears leak from their eyes, from the eyes of their children, and the mothers drive away in cars packed with clothes and bedding and the things they can't live without.

Water seeps from the cracks in our roads like bleeding wounds. *It looks like the Earth is crying*, someone says. *Aren't we all*, we say.

We light candles at night despite the heat. We set them on tables made steady with books and coasters. The radio tells us of homes burned down by candles that slid from mantels.

We blow out the candles.

We stand in the street together. Smell the smoke. Hear the sirens. The dogs have all gone quiet.

We point at our new sky—so many more stars than we ever thought possible, so we set up lawn chairs on tilted drives and walks, and we talk to each other in tight voices and wonder if we should worry about looters. *They say it's begun in East County*. We share the food our refrigerators can no longer keep cold and listen to the water that bubbles up and heads west—our city's reserves run toward the sea. We sip warm beer and say, *So this is the Big One. Is this what the end feels like?*

Feeding Strays

Greer pulled a strip of rubbery, partially chewed chicken from her mouth and tossed it onto the saggy porch.

"I wouldn't do that," said a distracted voice beside her. Rita—her closest friend slash latest boss—eyed the gray tabby eyeing the meat, then dove once more into the cold rotisserie chicken sitting on the side table between them. She'd been excavating the carcass for a while now, cracking bones and flicking bits of rubbery tendon at Greer between pauses in the half-hearted small talk.

Greer toed the meat toward the cat. "It's too tough. Hurts my jaw."

"That's why I go for the dark meat. It's easier to chew when it's cold." The tabby crouched over the masticated meat, sniffed it, and then purring, ate it.

"I fed a stray once and it showed up yowling every night for almost a year," said Rita.

Greer ran a hand along the tabby's spine. "He's sweet." To her all animals were male until they proved otherwise. "And besides," she said, "he probably has an owner near here. You take everything so serious."

Rita laughed. "You'll see, girly."

"Even so. It might be nice to have some company at night. This neighborhood is too quiet."

"I bet. No one yelling at you, calling you stupid or giving you bruises. Must be a real drag."

"It was someone to cook for."

"Jezus, Greer."

Rita slid a paper grocery bag toward her. "Let me know if there's anything you don't want."

The bag held a can of tuna days away from expiration, three severely dented cans of New England clam chowder, a rusty head of iceberg lettuce . . .

Greer held up a bag of tortilla chips. "Why are these open?"

"A stock boy found it on the shelf like that."

"The pothead one, you mean?"

The sun had set and the air began to cool. Summer had ended weeks ago, but Greer shivered with this first nip of fall. The whirligigs would start up any day now, just before the maple leaves began to turn. She tore another strip off the bird for the cat. It ate again. She leaned forward and dropped her hand. The cat came to her, sniffed, then pressed its head into her palm and leaned its body against her leg.

"Just promise me that if Jeff comes around, you won't feed him too," said Rita.

"What would I even make, a tuna fish tortilla chip casserole?"

"There's more than one way to feed a man, G."

"I'm off men for the next year."

Greer had made declarations like this before. To Rita. To anyone who'd listen.

"Have you ever gone a year without one?"

"You make it sound like going without a shower or toothpaste or *vodka*."

Rita didn't laugh. "When was the last time you went more than a week without a man around?"

She thought a moment. Jeff had been two and a half years, before that Todd had been three, Jeremy one . . . *what did it matter anyway?* If anything, her relationship history proved her loyalty and . . . and work ethic for Chrissake.

Rita continued, "Why don't you try dating—as in, go on a date with someone and then never see or speak to them again—like the rest of us? Or at least decide whether or not you actually *like* a person before going out again."

Greer wanted to say, "What's not to like?" but instead vapidly stroked the cat's back and counted the bits of green growing in the rot between the porch boards. *Two, three, plus three, six, seven* . . . Without warning the cat pinned its ears, spun around, and swatted her hand. Greer yelped, more in surprise than pain. The cat darted off the porch and around the side of the duplex. She put her hand to her lips, and when she showed it to Rita, two red lines had already started to welt, though no blood came to the surface.

Rita shook her head. "That cat's an asshole. If he comes back, don't feed him."

"He was just trying to play—you really do take everything so serious."

Greer works at a small grocery store two miles away. Rita got her the job when she was promoted to assistant manager—when Greer finally decided she needed to leave Jeff. Doing so meant she no longer worked as a clerk at the Jiffy Lube he co-owned, and so, thirty-eight and single again, she took Rita's offer. Like everything else in this world, the grocery store depresses her to no end. The lights are too yellow. The aisles are too cold. And until she started working there, she never realized how terrible it could be to find food where it doesn't belong. Salsa on the magazine rack. Beef jerky in the apple bin. Once she found a slab of raw steak, out of the package, in the middle of the ice cream aisle. She spent ten minutes crying in the employee bathroom after that one.

She enjoys mopping. Well, she enjoys pushing the bucket of soap-water around with the mop and has found that she can do laps around the store without anyone bothering her. Until yesterday, when the butcher held up a wet bag of shrimp and said, "These are gonna be tossed tonight, you want 'em?"

She shrugged and tried not to think about how depressed expired gift shrimp made her feel. Was it so obvious—her situation—to the rest of the world?

That night, while draining noodles to go with the shrimp, she heard a faint mew at the back door. Rita's voice in her head told her to ignore it. She opened a half-used jar of Alfredo sauce—intending to use the last of the milk to thin the congealed sauce, and perhaps have enough left to use another day.

The tabby jumped to the back of a patio chair and stared at her through the window. Its mews became louder, more aggressive—as if he were trying to pronounce *me-ow* one syllable at a time.

"Sorry, kid! I'm using the milk. You better scram," she said with her back to the window.

The cat leaped from the back of the chair and onto the window screen. It was hanging there by its claws, face pressed against the screen, eyes fixed on her, when the frame broke free of the window. She heard the crash and rushed outside to find the cat sitting tall and proper, as if expecting her and completely unashamed by his behavior. He looked up with round, dilated black eyes.

"Oh fine. You can have some." And she decided water would do just fine to thin the sauce. She stroked the cat's back for a moment, enjoying the rhythmic, mechanical purr while he drank. The calm was abruptly broken by the shrill scream of the smoke alarm going off in the house.

She'd left the burner on when she set the pot of strained noodles back on the stove, and now dark smoke rose from the pot. She put it in the sink and ran water over the mess, then opened the kitchen window and waved a dishrag at the smoke detector until it stopped.

When she turned around, the cat was on the kitchen counter licking its paw over the now empty shrimp plate. She threw her rag at him and shouted, "Shoo Goddammit!" but the rag didn't startle him. In fact, he looked at her with a sort of amused satisfaction. The damn thing was still purring.

"You need to go now," she said and reached for the cat. He was faster and reached right back, pulling her hand into his mouth. She cried out, this time in pain, and the cat bolted. The scratches from the day before now had a set of puncture wounds to complete the look. They were white at first, but unlike the scratches, blood seeped to the surface. She remembered hearing once that cat mouths and claws were riddled with dangerous bacteria, so she rummaged around under the bathroom sink until she found a bottle of expired hydrogen peroxide and poured it over her hand. She microwaved a frost-bitten curry dinner and went to bed.

Once, she had made the mistake of blocking one of Jeff's slaps and instead of a stinging face, ended up with a bruised and tender forearm. The feeling was similar now; she woke with a stiff, swollen hand. Greer pulled work clothes from a pile on the floor, squeezed the last of the mealy toothpaste onto her toothbrush, and reheated yesterday's coffee—all with her less dominant hand. She decided to walk rather than ride her bike to work—her hand so stiff she doubted she'd be able to squeeze the brake. It had rained some in the night and the morning air had that longed-for fall bite to it. She tucked her sore hand into the front pocket of her sweatshirt and cradled it gently with the other hand.

The butcher and the woman from produce stood smoking at the back entrance.

"How'd those shrimp turn out?" he asked. His food gifts always came with a follow-up. Sometimes she considered turning down the expired food, but she was in no place to turn down free *anything* right now.

"Wish I could tell you. A cat broke into my house and ate them."

He laughed. "A cat burglar, huh?" She smiled and nodded. Produce rolled her eyes—she could afford to not laugh at his stupid jokes.

Greer opened the heavy steel door between them, triggering the fly-fan. Before the door could close, Produce called out, "Hey, there was a guy asking for you."

She jammed her foot in the door; the fly-fan blasted her from above. Greer raised her eyebrows and waited.

"He just walked by a few minutes ago. Asked if you worked today," the butcher added.

"Did you catch a name?"

"Nah," said Produce, "but he was handsome in that scruffy kind of way. Big tattoo on his forearm."

Definitely Jeff. She'd figured he'd try to see her or contact her, eventually. It had been almost three weeks, and she had hoped the restraining order would do its job despite the nagging suspicion it could make things worse.

"What'd you tell him?"

"Said we didn't know, cuz we didn't know," she said with a shrug. Just before the door closed, she heard the butcher say, "Am I kinda scruffy?"

Greer went straight to the manager's office, stopped at the window, and waited to be waved in. Rita sat behind a gunmetal desk cluttered with papers and office knick-knacks, complete with a weepy-looking plant atop a stack of file folders. The room smelled like fermented fruit and soggy cardboard. The office had no central heating, and poor insulation made it as cold as the frozen food aisle; Rita had on a scarf and fingerless gloves.

"Can I take a half-day?" asked Greer.

Rita made a frowny face. "But I want my bestie here. My misery can't be complete unless I know you're suffering with me."

"Jeff came by."

Rita stood up and pulled down the blind of the office window—as if he were lurking somewhere in the building, spying from the cluttered hallway.

"He's not here now. At least, I don't think he is."

"What'd he want?"

"Don't know. But, look at this." She held up her wounded and swollen hand. It throbbed a little with the sudden movement.

Rita's eyes grew wide. "Did he do that to you? I'm calling the cops."

"No, it was that stupid cat."

Rita opened and closed three desk drawers before fishing out a used tube of antibiotic cream.

Rita covered the afternoon shift and Greer borrowed her car. A bobblehead of some character from a fantasy movie she'd never seen nodded from the dash while she adjusted the seats and mirrors, reminding her of the last time she'd been in Rita's car. A time when that fantasy-head had nodded at her in the passenger's seat while Rita drove her to the ER—the pain in her side so severe she could hardly breathe and thought she might be dying. *Am I dying? Am I dying?* And the nodding head just kept confirming that, *Yes, yes, you're dying.* Something was at least. Later the x-rays showed two broken ribs and a partially collapsed lung. She stayed on Rita's couch after that and by the next week, Rita had secured her the job at Season's Best and moved her into the duplex. Rita's cousin had been the former tenant. Thinking of it all now, Greer realized she probably owed Rita her life—the bobblehead nodded in confirmation of this too.

The doctor's cold fingertips massaged the lymph nodes in her neck. She asked, "Have you ever had a bad reaction to a cat bite or scratch before?"

She shrugged. None that she could remember.

The doctor lifted her hand and turned it over. "Did your cat do this?"

"No. It's just some cat that's been coming around. I thought he was someone's pet, but maybe he's feral. He's certainly unpredictable."

She felt self-conscious even though she knew that was silly.

"Well, I'm concerned about cat scratch fever here."

"That's real?"

"It is, and I'm putting you on a round of antibiotics. If you start to feel worse—cramping, muscle aches, fever—come back right away."

Jeff had never liked cats. He hated them actually, and Greer never really understood his contempt. He'd kept a BB gun by his front door and shot the cats that crept into his yard.

"They come over here and shit under the shrubs and then the neighbors' dogs come over and eat it," he'd told her. "It's a public nuisance." He laughed every time he hit one too.

"It's like that video game where you shoot the ducks," he'd said once, "only the cats jump up in the air, do back flips sometimes. Fuckin' hilarious."

She'd asked him not to shoot at them, she'd even grabbed the BB gun from him once, but that ended with a fat lip. She felt for the cats at the time, but as she forked over her co-pay for antibiotics, she could almost understand the desire to make a cat smart. Though Jeff had more hate in him than any cat—than probably any*one*—deserved.

She left Rita's car in the Season's Best parking lot and walked home in the fading light. The morning chill returned with the sundown. A scuff of feet behind her made her jump. Without turning around, she instinctively crossed the street.

Her thoughts went only to Jeff. How had he found out where she worked now? She did a quick glance over her shoulder. Whoever had been there hadn't crossed the road with her. Even so, she quickened her pace toward home. If Jeff found her, would she have to move somewhere new?

She could see the figure on the other side of the street now. Definitely a man, and she tried to convince herself that he wasn't intentionally keeping pace with her. From the corner of her eye, she could tell that he, whoever he was, had the hood of his sweatshirt pulled up. The streetlights began to turn on with tinny clicks. She stepped over a smattering of soggy whirligigs that had fallen under the maple at the corner and shuffled into the alley beside her landlord's house. Reggae and pot fumes floated out his open window. She followed the chipped flagstone path to her back porch door. She imagined him closing in. She fumbled the keys—her hand even more stiff with the sterile bandages tied around the wounds by an urgent care nurse. She entered the house and re-locked the door.

"Stop it," she said. "You're being paranoid."

Her phone chirped. She jumped in the dark of the kitchen.

A message from an unknown number read: *I miss you.*

It could only be him. She he had even changed numbers.

Another chirp with the message: *So. Much.* She tapped the cursor into the textbox and let it blink.

She flipped on the porch light and peered out the kitchen door window. The yard was empty.

She texted Rita: *You and T-Rex have any interest in a sleepover?*

Sometimes it feels as though she's floating over her life. And it's in those moments that she wonders if it's really herself—as she really is—that she's seeing, or if it's some kind of cosmic tease, like: *if you aren't careful, this is who you'll be.* Sometimes these moments are hopeful—that it can all be different. That the way she sees herself isn't the way other people see her. Those moments usually come after a couple of heavy pours, and for a while she thinks, she believes, that she is someone who will be happy. That she's almost there. And then other moments, like this one, she sees herself like this, crouched behind her kitchen door, a door she's only known for a couple weeks, in a cracker box she's only lived in for a couple weeks, and feels like this isn't her life. It can't be. She can't be someone she hates this much. She can't be someone this afraid. This sad. And either way, after moments like these, she wakes up with a hangover. That's how it goes.

She didn't turn on any lights until she heard the click of T-Rex's toenails on the porch. The dachshund paused at the door to jump on Greer—pawing at her knee with front legs just a little too short for his back ones.

She scratched his chest the way he liked. "Oh Rexy, you're so sexy."

"That line never gets old." Rita held a plastic bag containing her toothbrush and clean underwear for the morning. "Should I have brought my gun?"

"You don't have a gun."

"I have pepper spray."

"I'm being paranoid and just need company. You don't have to stay. Have you had dinner?"

Rita accepted her offer of a cold chicken salad wrap she'd pilfered from the Day Old stack in the deli, two days prior. The soggy tortilla broke apart in their hands. Greer found a packet of saltines, which they used to scoop out the chicken salad.

They ate mostly in silence, listening to the crunch of the stale crackers and the clicking of Rex's nails on the wood floor, his reconnaissance mission around the interior nearly complete.

A yowl came from the back porch. Rex let lose a high-pitched bark from the bathroom. The tabby sat crouched on the back of the porch chair.

"He's come to finish you off," said Rita. "I told you not to feed him."

"Well I definitely learned my lesson. That reminds me—" Greer pulled the antibiotic pills out of her bag and swallowed one with a swig of boxed chardonnay. She rinsed out a mason jar and poured a glass for Rita.

The cat made a kind of pathetic, mewing sound and rubbed the length of its body along the now screen-less window.

"I think he feels bad about the whole thing," said Greer.

Rex came tearing into the room, growling between barks. He lunged at the window. The cat startled and gracelessly leapt off the back of the chair, hit the railing of the deck with a thud, then disappeared into the shrubbery.

"See? Rexy knows an asshole when he sees one—why can't you?"

Greer went to the window. "You never know, he might be the abused one. Like the schoolyard bully who gets burned with cigarette butts at home—maybe that's his problem."

"The problem is you thinking up excuses."

Greer caught a glimpse of gray and white as it ducked under a hedge in the far corner of the yard. She felt a little sad seeing him slink away, rejected.

The next morning Greer emerged from her room to find that Rita and Rex had gone, their blankets folded neatly at one end of the couch. She put a mug of water in the microwave and removed the bandages from her hand while she waited. The swelling had gone down a little, maybe, and the throbbing had stopped, some. Purple and yellow bruises, like tiny pansies, had blossomed around each puncture wound. She took another pill with her lukewarm tea and went back to bed.

The cat woke her. He was yowling again. She checked the clock on her phone, four in the afternoon. She'd slept through her work shift and had five messages from Rita asking first if she planned to come in, then annoyed by her lack of response, then worried if she was okay. Greer responded: *Sorry. In bed. Feel awful.* And she did. She didn't own a thermometer, but she shivered, and her reflection in the bathroom mirror confirmed it: pale, sweaty, glassy-eyed. Not good.

The cat called again. He was in his spot, rubbing against the kitchen window. His eyes followed her while she made more tea and slouched around the kitchen for something to eat. She swatted fruit flies off a brown banana, decided she wasn't hungry. She found one of the expired cans of tuna behind some rice that had a pantry moth fluttering around at the top of the bag.

The cat watched her with its round, black eyes. His cries were soft and mewling; she could hear his purring through the thin window. He did love her, she thought, he just didn't know how to show it.

She set the tuna by the back door and crouched in the doorway, stroking his back as he ate, then closed and locked the door before he finished and could ruin the moment. She lifted the blind on the kitchen door window. Jeff stood at the bottom of the porch steps, his hands shoved deep into his front pockets. He shrugged and flashed a half smile.

She snapped the blinds down again and crouched below the window knowing—and at the same time rejecting—the idea that he'd seen her. And, maybe he hadn't been there at all. Maybe she'd imagined it. Her stomach cramped and sweat broke out on her forehead.

Then came footsteps on the porch, back and forth, back and forth. Footsteps that made the porch creak.

"GiGi, open the door. I'm sorry. I want you to come home." He moved to the window above the kitchen sink; she could hear him press his face against it.

"I can't do any of it without you. I'm dying here. Can't we talk?" He paced again. The tuna dish went skidding across the planks. He swore. She willed her body to stay quiet, to not betray her. She mouthed the words, *Don't feed him, don't feed him, don't feed him* while he yowled outside the door.

Every Version of Me

The tombstone reads:
Sis died, and you didn't cry.
May 1992

I hit the raw earth with my shovel then pick my way around the others, back toward the house. The spadework has shot my posture right to hell. Though, to be fair, my father used to call me Quasi and pinch the skin between my shoulder blades until I stood straight enough—so maybe it was never that great to begin. Either way, this is not how I planned to spend my golden years: digging and burying, redigging and reburying, but what choice do I have? Can't exactly let Myself run around the neighborhood willy-nilly half-dressed half the time, now can I?

I'm not sure how much longer I'll be able to keep it up, though. It's tempting sometimes to crawl down into one of these holes I dig and wait for the darkness to come, for some kind of peace to descend, or at least for a little nap that lasts more than an hour. Take today, for instance: no sooner do I roll the kinks out of my neck and scrub the dirt from under my yellow nails than there's a familiar *knock-knock-knock* on the kitchen door.

I know it's Me even though I don't recognize Myself—at least not right away—standing there, stinking and dripping all over my doormat, clumps of musky, wet earth crammed in the corners of My eyes, in the folds of My ears, in the crannies of My worm-munched skin. This particular Me is wearing nothing but an oversized T-shirt, and I think, *I remember those legs*, and you know?—they still look pretty good. Putrefied flesh and all.

I recognize the shirt, despite the holes and rot stains. Even an old, forgetful thing like me can see it's Mick Jagger's iconic mouth. The shirt belonged to my first husband before it became my nightshirt. I haven't thought of this Me in decades, nor of the man that shirt belonged to. A different life ago, and yet all it takes is a stupid shirt with fungal lips and fetid holes like canker sores to bring back all those nights spent with it pushed up and everything going down, and ravenous mornings when, half asleep, he'd reach for me, and I'd shiver as his hand crawled its way up under it, staking claim to a breast. I shiver now to think of it, but for a thousand different reasons, for a thousand different hurts. I know the end of that story now and wonder how I ever convinced myself that *he'll be faithful this time, this time he'll stay clean, it's the music not him, it's only cocaine, he wouldn't hit you again.* But the next thing you know, you're packing a bag in the dead of night while he's passed out in the bathroom; when his drummer looks up at you from his line on your coffee table, you tell him and his prostitute, "Going out for cigarettes," but really you go to the police station to show some skeptical, dead-faced cop your eye and cheek and back. Eventually you get a restraining order against your own husband and wonder when exactly the one who was supposed to love and protect you became the one you feared most in the world.

There were some quiet, kind moments before and in between, of course. Moments that made you stay longer than you should have. When you talked about the future and where you'd live and how many kids you'd make. Before the restraining order, before he got behind the wheel and killed that family of four, that family on their way home from goddammed El Torrito. They just wanted dinner, and he just wanted *you*. He *killed them* and blamed you for leaving, and for his sentence, and for moving on.

"You look like shit," I say to Me and feel just as lost and alone as I did all those years ago. I step aside so I can enter.

I've tried everything, or nearly everything, to get Myself to stay in my graves. The first time one of Me showed up, I opened the door to an eleven-year-old child. The rotting, reeking little thing blinked until I, in my horror, finally understood who she was, who she had been. I hadn't thought of her—of Me—in so long. I curled up on the couch and cried, "I'm sorry," while she—while I—sat rigid on the other side, clumps of dirt falling from mud-matted hair and hitting the couch cushions with the consistent patter of rainfall. I fell asleep and when I woke, it was to my husband—my second husband, Stan . . . Good Stan . . . Saint Stan—brushing mud off the far end of the couch.

I told him I thought I'd buried her five hundred miles away, way back when, but she found me. It was his idea to rebury the child. Said he'd take care of it, the way he always took care of me, and that I didn't have to think about what that man did to her anymore—not if I didn't want to. So, from the kitchen window, I watched as he dug up a chunk of lawn in his work slacks and penny loafers, the sleeves of his white shirt rolled up and his tie tucked between two buttons with nothing but the flickering porch light to guide his shovel. He laid Me to rest, and for a moment, when that leggy little version of me hesitated at the edge of that grave, I felt a twinge of guilt sending her back into the dark.

Not one version of Me showed up at the back door for ten years after that—for as long as Saint Stan lived. But, the day after I laid him in the ground . . . I had no idea so many had been lying in wait.

I was angry. So angry at first. I yelled at them. Screamed, even— so loud the neighbors called the Sheriff once. I tried to ignore the knocks, left Myself swaying, vapid and catatonic, on the back steps in fog or rain or sun. I begged Me to go away, to stay in the earth, to stop all this—what was this even? This haunting. This agonizing exhumation. I tried to reason with Me: Aren't you tired? Don't you want *to rest in peace?* But nothing stops the knocking. At least nothing I've found yet. No matter how many holes I fill, there is always a Me ready to claw her way to the surface of a grave I don't remember digging in the first place.

"Chamomile?" I ask Myself.

I shake My gory locks and remember I used to drink black coffee back then, with maybe a little whiskey to sweeten. I watch Me move, stiff and creaking, to the kitchen table. I sigh at the muddy footprints. The dirt is never-ending.

"What can I do for you?" I say and wait for a response that isn't coming. I have a new theory, though, that if I can just tell Me what I want—or need—to hear, then I'll go to the grave with a little less fuss and a little more ease.

I place a cup of cold black coffee left over from the morning's brew in front of Me.

"You know, I have other shit to do." I don't, really, but I can't help it. I've been saying more of these mean things with a meanness I don't mean and can't control.

The rot isn't as bad as others I've seen, the stench not so much gag-inducing as stomach-clenching, and judging by what's left of the meat of Me, I'll probably be back a time or two before I stay properly buried. I want it and fear it. Other versions of Me are buried and gone. Like old pictures pulled from a wall, their remains are impressions left on faded wallpaper; I can see the shape but not the image anymore.

But when I show up like this, ragged and weary, fresh from the grave? The memories are palpable. The years spent in that Stones T-shirt sear like a branding iron—or one of Daddy's old Marlboros.

"Do you need to hear that it wasn't your fault?" God, that's all I ever want to hear, isn't it? Half my life is spent trying to convince Me it wasn't My fault.

And all the while I wonder, what if it *was* my fault and that's why I keep showing up? We weren't allowed to talk back then the way we do now, the way kids do today. Adults listen to kids now, maybe more than they should, but it's better than not at all. It's better to be alone and have a voice than a life that depends upon a man willing to give you one. Stan was the first man who ever listened to me, and then I secretly resented him for being the man who taught me how to be something I couldn't be on my own.

I struggle My purple, bloated fingers around the cold mug. Coffee splashes onto the Formica tabletop.

"Fine. It's not your fault he killed those people."

I stop with the mug and turn a pair of milky-white-coated eyes on me, and I know I'm asking for forgiveness I can't give. All I can hope is that once I get Myself under a mound of dirt again, I'll sink into that primordial muck and rejoin the tangle of corpses slowly becoming food, liquid, history, whatever, beneath the rest of us. Maybe this'll be the last time with one of Me. (I think this every time.) But, maybe it will be, and I can start moving forward without looking back.

I stand up.

I stand up too.

I follow Me to the backyard and take up the spade left leaning against the side of the house, beside tomato boxes I don't have time to fill. We pass the old graves, so many now that I tell my stepchildren, when they visit anymore, not to let their children play back here. I never leave an open grave, but even so. *What if they saw Me?*

Though many of the epitaphs have lost meaning to me, I can't help but look at the headstones as we pass.

You let them tease her, even at her funeral.
September 1954–June 1956

He touched others, too, and you never said a word.
May 1955–January 1958

You felt nothing when they scraped her out of you.
July 1961

Sometimes I'm grateful I can't recall these details of my life anymore—the tombstones are blessings. I lift the shovel and give Me a poke in My squishy back, nudge Me on toward My grave. I find a new plot space, then fight shovelful after shovelful of black earth up out of the ground until I am wheezing, sweating. A fat earthworm rolls over in the soil, and then he's gone again.

"Well go on, and for *Chrissake* stay down there."

I resist the urge to give Me a kick as I'm struggling Myself down into the hole. Just once I'd like to watch Me tumble and break apart. I want to hate Me, but I don't—not today, anyway. And then I do it: this time, I climb down into the hole too. It isn't deep, but it is quieter than above. I shiver. I help Me lie down. It's awkward and cramped, but I can tell I'm grateful. I arrange what's left of My hair and place My hands over My heart. I say to Me, "I don't want to be forgotten either" and struggle myself out of the grave.

Once I have Me covered over, safe in the earth again, I give the mass a routine smack and stomp, even say a little prayer over My body.

You left, and they died instead of you.
October 1973

In the kitchen, I put the water on for another cup of honeyed tea. I consider other ways to spend my time. Knitting or needle-point—things women my age seem to enjoy. I used to paint a decent picture, I'm pretty sure, but these bright ideas are interrupted by three knocks on the kitchen door.

Guidelines and Tips for Becoming a Shooting Star

1. Remain calm.

You have purchased the *crème de la crème* of packages; don't squander the experience with a panic attack. So bridges make you sweat. So you chew three Xanax every time you board a plane. So you refused to open your eyes at the top of the Empire State Building, so so so . . . Think of the hospital beds and the tubes and the shots you will not have. Think of the chemo and the surgeries and the lopped-off body parts you're *not* trading for a few extra months. You've made your decision, so take deep, deliberate breaths of that beautiful oxygen cocktail pumping through your space suit and enjoy that drug-induced euphoria for the first (and last) time in your life.

2. Stay in the moment.

You will orbit Earth twice in roughly four hours before reentry. To make the most of your final hours, it is recommended that the first orbit be spent enjoying the view. Take it all in. Live those moments you forgot to take in life when you were too busy taking food-selfies, making loan payments, and getting yourself all worked up in that grass-is-always-greener/beat-the-Joneses lather of yours. And for once, let him go—he didn't destroy your life. Not all of it, anyway, so for the love-a-Pete don't think about that bastard. Instead, relish the sunrise and sunset—the ones you should have enjoyed from your front porch or the top of a mountain—the ones you will soon see from a rare and heavenly vantage. Don't lose your focus now.

Thanks to the in-suit navigation system, both natural and man-made phenomena such as the Grand Canyon, the Great Wall, the Great Pyramids—all the grands and greats—will be pointed out to you on the first orbit. The second orbit, slightly faster than the first, will be silent. It is at this time that the silence will make you wonder if you've died already. You'll try not to list your regrets, but you will. You'll try not to think of your missed opportunities, your weakest, most cowardly moments, but you will. Luckily, at that point, it's almost over.

3. Concerning the Sleep Option.

When you have experienced the second sunset, you will have approximately ninety seconds to press the *Sleep* button before free fall and combustion. Your coursework and orientation have informed you about reentry disintegration. Not that you need reminding, but burn up is inevitable and there are no take-backs. The speed of reentry, approximately seven kilometers per second, will turn you into a human fireball. A shooting star. You can use the Sleep Option at this time and miss the fiery pain of your own spectacle.

4. Remember, you're a Trailblazer here.

Oh, the curiosity of the living to see the end of others. Oh, the instinct of humans to look to others for guidance and reassurance and example. How we hope our journey to the other side isn't difficult. More eyes will be looking up at you, to be sure, than saw your fifth grade piano recital, your college graduation, or any of your weddings. Be brave for them, even if you're terrified. Hell, go out with a wave.

5. Let Go. Let OOM.

You'll be placed in an airlock and released at the Optimum Orbital Moment (OOM). You will want to reach for a safety rail and hold on and shout that you've changed your mind, but in the end, the vacuum of space will win and take your dignity with it. Don't let that happen. Resist the urge to grasp for more time. Hold your own hand if you must—it's always been just you, anyway, even if you thought it wasn't. Every one of us must go. Not one of us, for all our achievements, for all our fighting and raging and loving and growing, has ever been able to stay. If you can remember that, then the letting go will feel like the beginning.

A Fairytale Ending

At first, the hours flew by. We didn't notice when tonight turned to next morning and next morning to next day, and even now sometimes we forget. Servants doze where they stand. The musicians (the ones who are still here, anyway) take turns nodding off mid-song. Our feet won't stop. Our arms won't let go. We've become little more than ball bearings spinning around each other, our friction worn away. Woman and beast made man and wife.

When our wedding dance began, he said, "You take the weight off me," and I could have floated away. I wonder what he thinks of the weight of me now. We are paper thin, the two of us, held together by the frailest sinews of our story. Others around us have faded, crumbled one by one and forgotten. A couple hundred years will do that to most stories, but not ours, not yet. We dance on the dust of them. Some have tried to change us, but the ending is always the same, goddammit.

Sometimes I hate him. He smells of licorice root and lavender.

Sometimes I love him. He never steps on my feet.

Sometimes the sleeve of his jacket slides up his forearm, and as I turn beneath it, I glimpse the dark arm hair and remember the beast I fell in love with. I want him to rage, to break free of his body's borders, to shatter this ever after.

We smile because it's written, but our eyes have told a thousand other stories, have fought a thousand fights, have strayed a hundred thousand ways. We go round and round, and so does the world outside us.

The castle walls crumble a bit each day. They are giving in to the encroachment of vines and trees that slip twiggy fingers between cracks and crevasses and expand while we're busy shrinking. Mice emerge from hidden places and scamper across our wedding table. They sniff empty tureens, platters, and trays that once held soufflés, puddings, and cakes—spoils looted by their mousy ancestors so long ago. I watch the disappointed creatures leave again, disappear into the castle's living walls, and I envy them that freedom.

The skies have learned to roar, and strange shadows drift across the ballroom floor with us. All the bells have gone shrill—they've lost somehow that visceral vibration; they ring without feeling. We no longer hear the laughter of children playing on the castle lawns below—we hear whispers that they lock themselves into rooms and stare at glowing boxes all day long.

We dance and we dance.

We used to speak of our life together, after all this. But I see it in his eyes and I'm sure he sees it in mine. We fear it. We fear it as much as we fear this never-ending end. One day, perhaps when the world has spun its last, we will be forgotten and in turn, forget ourselves. Just as the guests, musicians, servants, *all* have slipped into the ether, so might we. It is the best we can hope for in this tormented bliss, in this loving hate, in this happily ever after and ever after.

Acknowledgments

Thank you Josh, Eva, and Steve—you all know why. Thank you *Hozier* for the haunting lyrics and melodies that inspired most of these stories. And, thank you Mom and Dad for telling me I could write in the first place.

Thank you to the editors, judges, and submissions committees of the following journals where stories from this collection first appeared, sometimes in slightly different form.

"When the Bees Come Back" first appeared in *Gemini Magazine* as the 2015 Flash Fiction Contest winner and was later nominated for a Pushcart Prize.

"The Big One" appeared in *Cease, Cows* (2017).

"Feeding Strays" won *pheobe*'s 2017 Fiction Contest judged by Patricia Park.

"Every Version of Me" appeared in *Front Porch Journal* (2017).

"A Fairytale Ending" appeared in *Flash Fiction Magazine* as "This Happily Ever After" (2016).

"Tips and Guidelines for Becoming a Shooting Star" appeared in *Streetlight Magazine* (2018).

Photo: Lyn Rosten

Ashley Morrow Hermsmeier holds an MFA in fiction from Pacific University. Her short stories, essays, and flash fiction have appeared in journals such as *phoebe*, *Michigan Quarterly Review*, *Flash Fiction Magazine*, *Streetlight*, *Front Porch*, *Weber*, and many others. She has won two previous fiction contests (2015, 2017) and is a Pushcart Prize nominee. She currently teaches English and writing in San Diego.